IT'S *Pucking* FAKE

DL GALLIE

This is a work of fiction, created without use of AI technology. Any names, characters, places or incidents are products of the author's imagination and used in a fictitious manner. Any resemblance to actual people, places, or events is purely coincidental or fictional.

Edited by **Karen Hrdlicka**, Barren Acres Editing
Man cover designed by **R.L. Kenderson**, R.L. Cover Designs
Alternate cover designed by **Kristie,** Vanilla Lily Designs and Pre-mades
Proofread by **Lisa Edwards**
Formatting and interior design by **DL Gallie**

Surrounded by sleazy men and desperate puck bunnies, Jett Jensen, New York Crusher's left wing, and I become each other's saviour. Fake dating at events is the game, and saving each other from awkward situations is the goal.

However, the rules change when Jett takes me as his date to his sister's wedding. It's hard not to be swept away in the moment and the romance of a Valentine's Day ceremony.

Our fake relationship suddenly becomes more real than either of us expected. Between whispered confessions and slow dances, our fate is sealed.

Until the next wedding…

MARGOT

With a less-than-friendly smile at the slimeball next to me, I turn and stare into my beer on the bar. Gripping the glass in my hand, I imagine pulling my arm back and throwing the glass, not the beer, in this jerk's face. I've lost count of how many times I've said I'm not interested, but it's like talking to a brick wall.

"So, what do you say ...?" he asks again, but this time he runs his finger along my forearm.

A shudder runs through me, and he mistakes it for lust and not the disgust it actually is, but before I end up wearing orange, someone slides up beside me. They pull me into them, and my eyes widen when I hear a, "Sorry I'm late, baby, practice ran over." And they widen farther when my mystery man places a kiss on my temple.

Great, another slimeball, I think.

Turning my head toward the person invading my personal space, I'm ready to unleash on them, but when I see who it is, I smile and relax. Jett Jensen is grinning at me. He's a player on the same team as my best friend's partner, and if I'm honest, I've always found him kinda cute.

He winks and silently gives me a 'just go with it' look, but before I can reply and continue the fake ruse, Mr. Slimeball interrupts, "Fuck off, dude, I was here first." He snickers at Jett. He clearly doesn't get I'm not interested or that Jett is my—fake— boyfriend.

Before I can put this asshole in his place once and for all, Jett steps between us. "Actually," Jett begins, "that's where you are wrong."

"What the fuck do you know? You just got here, asshole."

Rolling my eyes, I shake my head, this guy really is a dumbshit. It's no wonder he's single.

Jett's shoulders rise. "Actually ..." he repeats, and I get the feeling he's about to let loose on Mr. Slime- ball, but I want the honor of putting this douche in his place. After all, it's the twenty-first century, and

I'm a capable woman who can look after myself ... just not when it comes to spiders or birds.

"Excuse me," I say, tugging on Jett's arm. He looks back at me and sees the expression on my face. Nodding, he steps back, and Mr. Slimeball smirks at Jett. With him preoccupied, I pick up *his* beer and throw it in his face.

"What the fuck?" he growls. He jumps up and the seat he was sitting on tips over and crashes to the floor. "You fucking bitch." He sneers at me, wiping off his face.

"Watch your mouth," Jett hisses.

"That bitch just threw my beer at me."

"And that bitch," I voice, "thinks you deserved it. No means fucking no, you fucking slimeball."

"Whatever!" he shouts, throwing his hands in the air. "The bitch is all yours," he snaps at Jett. Shoulder-barging Jett, he begins to walk away just as security arrives, and they not so graciously escort him from the building after I fill them in on what is happening.

"You okay?" Jett asks after bending down to pick up the chair that was knocked over in the kerfuffle just now.

"Fine ... just sick of slimeballs who don't take no for an answer."

"Well, now that you're safe, I'll leave you to it."

"Wait," I call out, grabbing his arm, "sit and let me buy you a drink. You are my boyfriend, after all. It's the least I can do after you saved me from the slimeball dragon."

"Are you sure?"

"Positive ... besides, if you sit with me, it will stop the slimeballs from hitting on me."

"So, you just want me for my protection?"

Shrugging, I smile at him, take my seat again, and signal to the bartender for two more beers. Having a drink with a hot hockey player is not a bad way to end the night.

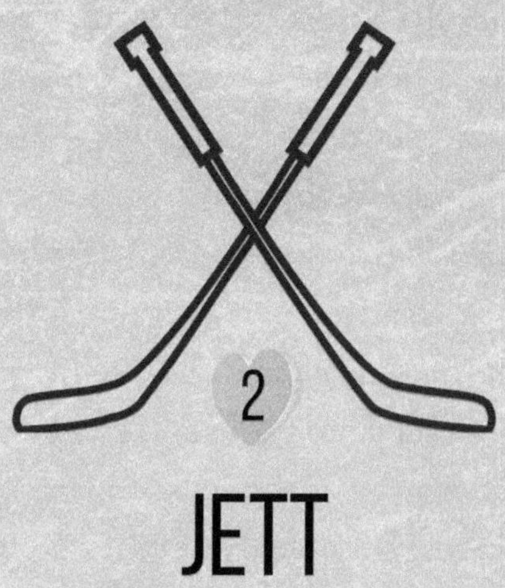

JETT

"You're not getting any younger, Jett," my mother says as if I'm a forty-year-old man and not the twenty-nine-year-old I am, but to be honest, I was wondering when this lecture would start.

It's the same thing every time we catch up. Don't get me wrong, my parents are great, amazing in fact, but my mom wants me to settle down. She wants me to give her grandbabies because by the time she was my age, she was married and had four boys, with twin girls on the way. Mom finally got the girls she was after—but unfortunately for her, Sadie and Olivia are not girly girls. Yep, I'm one of six and let me tell you, it was hectic growing up in the Jensen household, but I wouldn't change a thing. Well, except for maybe Shaun and his ass. If farting was an Olympic sport, he'd have several gold medals.

Do I want the whole family thing? Sure, one day, but not right now. Right now, I want to focus on my career and live footloose and fancy-free. I'm currently at the top of my game. My team is smashing it this season, and there's always a willing young lady to keep me warm at night, but I've yet to find anyone worthy of the Jensen name so I'll keep looking ... as tough as that may be.

My family has always supported me, and they try to come to as many games as possible, but life sometimes gets in the way.

Tonight was a home game, so Mom, Dad, and Olivia, one of my sisters, came into the city to watch. We smashed the LA Legends, 5-1. Winning is always great, but when we smash Doucheman's team, it's even sweeter. He used to be a player on our team, but he screwed over the coach's daughter and then was a douche to her new man, who just so happens to be our star goalie. Thankfully, he was traded to the LA team this season and he's no longer our problem.

He's not as douchey anymore, thanks to his Wren, his keeper/PR lady. She must be a witch to be able to tame the wild beast that is Stefan Däuchmen.

She's gotta have magical powers or something, but then again, underneath his doucheness, he's a pretty good guy. Well, he was until the fame of being an NHL player got to his head.

"Jett, are you listening to me?" Mom snaps.

"Yes, Mom, I am, and like the last million times we've had this conversation, I'm fine. I'm not ready for the grave just yet and I'm happy being single."

"But—"

"Nope, no buts, Mom. I'm happy, and when Mrs. Jensen comes into my life, you will be the first to know. Now, let's enjoy dinner." *Then I can meet up with the guys and find a puck bunny to take home because finding 'the one' isn't high on my to-do list right now.*

"You know I worry about you," Mom says, and from the tone she just used, I kind of feel bad for how I just spoke to her.

Reaching over the table, I squeeze her hand. "And I appreciate it, but, Mom, I'm twenty-nine years old and a starting player on an NHL team. I'm doing pretty good at this life thing, thanks to you and Dad. And guess what?"

"What?"

"I can even wipe my own ass."

"Jett," she admonishes me and slaps me on the arm. "That was uncalled for."

"Then leave the boy alone, Sara," Dad pipes in. "The right girl will come along when he least expects it, and then we can add another seat around the already cramped dinner table."

With having six kids, it was always tight at dinnertime. Add in five partners—yes, I'm the only single Jensen child—and now it's really squishy. I can only imagine what it's going to be like when we all start having kids, but if I'm honest, I can't wait to be an uncle ... and one day a dad.

The rest of the night goes smoothly, and as I'm sitting in the back of a cab—after dropping the family off at the train station to take them back to Jersey—I start thinking about the future and wonder if maybe it's time to start looking for 'the one'.

3
MARGOT

Sighing, I look around the bar and realize that once again, I'm the only single one in the room. Don't get me wrong, I love being single, but just once, it'd be nice to arrive at a party with someone. Then again, if I do that, I can't find some random hottie to hook up with and have a wild night between the sheets before we each go our separate ways.

I'm all for casual hookups. I don't need a man to weigh me down, I'm perfectly fine on my own. Besides, I'm only twenty-five, there's still plenty of time to find Mr. Margot, get married, and have babies, right?

As I sip on my margarita, I start to wonder why that is the definition of a happy life. Maybe being single and carefree is the secret to a happy life, but then I look at my best friend and the love of her life, and I get it. In all the years I've known Chels, I have never seen her happier than she is right now, and it's all due to Kallen Jones. The player who swept her off her feet and is giving her the happily ever after she deserves.

"Why do you look like your dog just died?" Jett asks as he takes a seat next to me.

"Because it did," I deadpan with a straight face, and it's soooo hard not to laugh at the expression on his face right now. My dog, Fluffy—don't ask, I was seven when I named him—did die ... when I was fifteen and my older brother, Ben, ran him over the day he got his driver's license.

"Ohh shit," he backpedals, resting his hand on my knee and squeezing. "I'm so sorry for your loss."

A laugh slips out. "Thanks but Fluffy died when I was fifteen and my brother accidently ran him over."

"You named your dog Fluffy? What type was it? A poodle?"

"No, Fluffy was an Australian shepherd. She had the fluffiest coat, hence her name."

"Well, I'm sorry for your loss when you were a teen, but why the sad face now?"

Looking over at him, I'm compelled to spill how I feel, so I do. "I realized that I'm once again the only single one. Chels has Kallen, JJ and Lexi are whatever the hell they are—"

"Those two just need to fuck and get back together."

My head snaps toward Jett and my eyes widen. "What do you mean back together?"

"It's a long story."

"Well, it's an open bar and I need the goss, now spill."

"Let me get us fresh drinks and I'll fill you in. Margarita, right?" He nods to my empty glass, and I confirm with a head tilt.

Spinning around, I watch as he walks over to the bar in the corner. A smile hits me when I realize he knows if I'm not drinking beer by the gallon my drink of choice is a margarita.

While he has his back to me, I take a moment to appreciate his jeans-clad ass.

What I would give to get a view of his gluteus maximus up close.

He returns a few moments later and hands me my cocktail. Bringing the straw to my mouth, I wrap my lips around it and sip. Closing my eyes, I savor the flavor and slightly moan.

"Shall I leave you and your margarita alone?"

"Ha," I chortle. "I'm good, but you can spill the tea on JJ and Lex."

"Right, okay, well, they were childhood sweethearts, and from the little I know, JJ fucked up and Lex vowed to never trust him again. JJ is still ass-over-tit in love with her, and I think he's starting to wear her down. If I can see the sparks, there's something there. I mean, I'm not the brightest when it comes to love. Hell, I didn't even know Kal and Chels were a thing."

"Seriously? Those two pretty much had a neon sign saying, 'we're banging' flashing all over the place."

"Well, after the Doucheman saga, I thought she'd sworn off players."

"She had, but they hooked up before he was officially on the team so technically ..." I leave that sentence open because what else is there to say? They banged, he joined the team, and she said, 'Thanks for a good night, that's it,' but that Canadian fell for my bestie, and he won her over. I'm so happy for her, especially after the way Stefan Däuchmen treated her. "But getting back to Lex and JJ, that's some history there, and after knowing what I now know, I'd bet my left tit that they'll be together in a matter of weeks."

"You're offering your tits as a wager?"

"It's not a real wager, so yeah, why not?"

"Well, if you don't mind me saying, you do have nice tits, and anyone would be lucky to win them."

"Why, thank you for admiring the girls. Lola and Lala appreciate the compliment."

"You've named your tits?"

Nodding, I cup the girls in my palms and give them a squeeze. Jett's eyes drop to my chest, and my cheeks heat at the intensity of his gaze.

"Why are you fondling Lola and Lala in a bar?" Chels asks, as she and Kallen join us.

"Who's Lola and Lala?" Kallen questions, slightly confused as there are only the four of us here.

"My tits," I reply, while Jett says, "Her tits."

Kallen and Chels dart their eyes between us before Kal drops his gaze to my chest, then quickly averts his eyes so Chels doesn't whack him for ogling another girl's tits.

"Do we even want to know?" Chels asks.

"Nope," Jett and I reply in unison. Then we both crack up laughing.

"Why do I get the feeling you two are going to be trouble?" Kallen states rhetorically. He pulls Chels into his chest, protectively resting his palm on her stomach, and if she didn't have a cocktail in her hand, I would think my bestie was keeping secrets from me.

"I don't know what you mean, Kallen Jones," I sweetly reply, but my gaze flicks to Jett, and I begin to wonder what mischief the two of us could get up to together.

4

JETT

"I need to know if you're bringing someone, Jett?" my sister growls at me through the phone.

"Why do I need to bring a date to your wedding, Sadie?" *Maybe I want to hook up with a bridesmaid … then I remember who they are and forget that plan.* "And why the hell is it on Valentine's Day? And why do you need to know so far in advance?"

"Weddings take time to plan. The date is because it's the day of love, and it also happens to be the day Ricky and I officially started dating."

"That's kinda sweet," I tell my sister.

"It is, right? Now, will you have a date? And before you tell me you don't need one, you should know Mom has insisted I invite Lisa Caldwell, as she wants to set the two of you up."

"Not again," I groan and shake my head. My mom has been trying to set me up with every single woman she knows in Jersey.

"Yes, again, and you know, if you just settled down, you wouldn't have to put up with this shit."

"I'm twenty-nine, Sade, not ninety-nine and ready for the grave. I don't get why all the women in my family want me to settle down." And to make my point, I reiterate, "Twenty-nine. Two nine."

"And as your baby sister, I'm getting married and you're not. People are going to start to wonder if you're gay." She pauses. "You're not, are you?"

"If I say yes, will you all go away and let me live my life?"

"Hell no, and we both know that will just open up a whole new conversation about you keeping secrets from your family." Then she adds, "And you and I both know that if you *are* gay, Mom will just try to set you up with Adam Caldwell instead of Lisa, and if that doesn't work, she'll start with the rest of the single gay men around here."

"Fuck my life," I mumble.

When I look up, I see Chels and Margot walk into Squires. Margot waves and I wave back. She nods to the bar and mimes *do I need a drink*, but I shake my head and lift my full water. Yep, I'm on the hard stuff tonight.

"Leave it with me and I'll get back to you."

"You have till the end of the month or I'm telling Mom to set you up with Lisa ... or Adam."

"Ugh, I hate you," I whine.

"No, you love me."

"Yes, yes I do love you, Sadie ... and I'm so happy you found Ricky."

"Me too," she agrees, and I hear nothing but love in her tone. "He is pretty great. I did well in the husband-to-be department, and the things that man can do with his—"

"Bye, Sadie!" I shout, interrupting her. I do *not* need to know what my sister's fiancé can do that makes her go gaga.

Just as I hang up, Margot arrives at the table. "What's up, Jensen?" she says by way of greeting.

"Not much. How's things, Radclyff?"

"It's two-for-one cocktails, so I'm grand. I see you're on the hard stuff this evening."

"Having a quiet one tonight."

"Still struggling from the weekend?"

"No, if you must know, my knee took a pretty hard hit in the game on Sunday, and I'm on some hard-core painkillers right now. I'm behaving so I'm all good for the game this weekend."

"Shit, you okay?"

Nodding, I rub at my knee. "Fine, just par for the course."

"Is my girl Lex looking after you?"

"Of course, she's the best at what she does."

"Who's the best?" Kallen asks, joining us.

"Lexi," I tell him.

"Don't let JJ hear you praise his woman, he'll beat your ass."

"I'd like to see him try. These guns ..." I lift my arms and flex, "... could take him on any day."

"Settle down, Stallone," Kallen teases while at the same time, Margot reaches out and squeezes my biceps.

Her eyes widen, and she says, "Holy muscles, Batman."

"Let me feel," Chels pipes in, earning herself a growl from Kallen.

"You touch his arm, and I'll spank your ass when we get home."

"That's not a punishment," Margot says, shocking me with her words.

"I didn't realize you were into that."

"There's a lot you don't know about me, Jett Jensen."

"Why does that not surprise me?" I tell her, taking a moment to stare at her. Something passes between us, but the moment is interrupted when a swarm of girls enter the bar and make a beeline for us.

"What do you say, should we head to the bathrooms, and I'll blow you?" the puck bunny next to me coos. I've been ignoring her all night, but she's not taking the hint.

Right now, she's leaning on the bar next to me. It's causing her tits to spill out of the top of her shirt and she's batting her eyelashes at me. She's trying to be seductive, but to be honest, she looks like she's having a seizure or a stroke or maybe a bug flew into her eye.

I love playing hockey, but this is the one part of the job I hate. However, it's a small price to pay for being paid millions to do what I do.

I'm about to shoot her down—again—when an

arm slides around my waist. I shudder, but when I look over my shoulder and see who it is, I smile. "Sorry it took forever to pee. Why are there only ever two stalls in places like this?"

"Who the fuck are you?" the bunny screeches.

Leaning around me, she raises her eyebrows at the bunny, not cowering at the murderous glare coming from the bunny. "Margot. Who the fuck are you?" she throws back.

"Umm, I was here first," the bunny sniggers at Margot, "and kindly remove your arm from around him. He's mine."

"Actually, sweetheart." Margot drops her arm from around my waist. She shimmies herself between me and the bar to face the bunny, Kandy, I think she said her name is. "Jett's mine. Now take your fake-ass extensions and plastic lips away from us."

"Are you going to let her talk to me like that?" the bunny asks me, ignoring Margot.

"Don't talk to him," Margot snaps. "Do you think it's okay to go around manhandling players and demanding they let you blow them? Have some class and show them respect. They're human just like you and I are. Now, if you excuse us, I'm going to blow my boyfriend in the bathrooms."

She laces her fingers with mine and pulls me away, but not before the bunny not so softly hisses, "What a fucking slut." I can't help but laugh because she proposed the exact same thing not two minutes ago.

When I look up, I realize Margot is leading us toward the restrooms. "Ummm, Margot, where are we going?"

"Bathroom," she says like that answers everything.

"What the fuck for?"

"To make bitchy bunny jealous."

"And why do we want to do that?"

She stops and turns to face me. "Because the killer scowl on her face right now is priceless, and I want to give her something to really be sour about. Now, follow me into the bathroom corridor and let me fake blow you."

5

MARGOT

Stepping into the bathroom corridor, I lead us past the restrooms and around the corner. Pushing the handle, I open the 'Staff Only' door. The lock clicks shut behind us, and when I turn to face Jett, my heart races as I stare at him.

In the dim lighting of the staff room, I study the man before me. His blond hair is styled in that messy but put-together way. His eyes are a vibrant green in this light, and I can see flecks of gold around the pupils. His tongue darts out and slides across his bottom lip, and I find myself doing the same before biting on mine.

He lifts his head, his gaze locked on mine, and we silently stare at one another.

The temperature increases.

My heart rate speeds up even further.

Swallowing deeply, I rapidly blink, but the moment is broken when the door opens and in walks the bar manager, Slade. "Margot, what are you doing in here?"

"Just needed a moment," I tell him.

Getting caught in a no-go area of my favorite bar with a hockey player is not on my to-do list for tonight, or ever. Thankfully for us, the door is hiding Jett so it looks like it's just me here. Therefore, we're safe ... ish.

"Do I need to kick someone's ass?" Slade asks, turning into the protective guy he's known to be. He steps toward me and towers his six-foot frame over me.

"Please," I scoff, "you and I both know I can handle myself."

"Tell me about it. If you ever want to leave being a graphic design wiz, come and see me and I'll give you a job as a bouncer."

"Thanks, but I think I'll stick with what I know. I'm more of a lover than a bouncer. What are you doing back here?"

"Heard that a bunny was gonna blow someone—"

"And you thought you'd get in on the action?" I throw a wink his way, and he chuckles. "Who knew you were so kinky?"

"You ain't seen kinky, Margot. The things I could show you ... again."

And show me he did, once, and normally I'd be ready to climb him like a tree again, but with Jett hiding behind the door, it's not really appropriate. And what's more shocking to me is I'd rather be kinky with Jett. *What's with that?* Sure, he and I have saved each other from bunnies and slimeballs recently, but it's nothing, we're just friends. Faking it to help each other out of a bind.

"You couldn't handle more of me, Slade, but I could do with another drink ... think you can hook a girl up?"

"That's a shame, but I respect that no means no, and yes, I can hook you up." He pauses. "And just so you know, you can ask me for anything anytime." He places emphasis on the word anything, and I can't help but be embarrassed as to what he's alluding to because Slade, I-don't-know-his-last-name is a freak in the sheets ... and against the wall ... and in the shower ... and on planet Earth.

"Noted ... now, let's get me a drink."

"Let's ... and, Jett, I'll have a mineral water waiting for you."

My eyes widen, and my mouth drops open at what Slade just said. "You're a jerk," I berate him, slapping him in the chest as I walk toward him and the door.

Pulling the door away from Jett, I stare at a just-as-shocked-as-me Jett. "Come on, Jensen, let's go get our free drink."

The rest of the night flies by and Slade gives me more than one freebie, Chels too.

Last drinks are called, but Kallen cuts the two of us off, spoilsport, but it's probably a good thing because I'm a wee bit tipsy right now.

We finish our drinks and then Chels, Kallen, Jett, and I head outside and wait for a cab.

There's a chill in the air and I shiver.

Before I know it, Jett wraps his arm around me and pulls me into his side. I'm accosted by Jett's scent. It's a mix of ice, leather, and mint. A shiver runs through me again, and he pulls me in closer.

"Thanks," I whisper as I burrow closer to him for warmth.

Finally, a cab arrives and the four of us climb in.

We drop Chels and Kal off first, and then I give

the driver my address and we head toward my place. My eyes become heavy, and I rest my head on the window and drift off to sleep.

The last thing I remember is Jett lifting me out of the cab. "This isn't my place," I mumble, and then I'm floating, wrapped in Jett's embrace.

6

MARGOT

There's a pounding in my head, and my mouth feels like a dirty ashtray. A dry, dirty ashtray because my tongue gets stuck to the roof of my mouth. Rolling to my side, I open my eyes and glance around the room, trying to figure out where I am.

I don't recognize this bedroom.

I don't recognize this bed and sheets.

Sitting up, I furrow my brows when I see I'm in a Crushers shirt. "I wasn't wearing this last night," I whisper. I catch a glimpse of my reflection and my eyes widen. I look like I feel, like shit.

"Damn you, Slade, and your free drinks," I grumble as I rub my temple to ease the throbbing.

My stomach rumbles, aka churns, and my

bladder lets me know it's full. Climbing out of the bed, I make my way into the attached bathroom and use the toilet. After flushing, I wash my hands and splash some water on my face. Staring at my reflection, I shake my head but instantly regret it when the room begins to spin.

Leaning down, I cup my hand and swish water around my mouth before I take a drink. I feel somewhat human after doing that.

Running my fingers through my hair, I make myself semi-presentable and then head out of the bedroom in search of a clue as to where I am and who I'm with.

Stepping into the living room, my eyes widen when I look at the sofa and see a sleeping Jett Jensen. His arm is splayed over his face, and a pair of gray sweatpants sit low on his hips.

Holy sculpted abs, Batman.

Stopped in the middle of the room, I stand here and ogle his body. Then I freeze when I realize his eyes are open and he's just caught me ogling him.

My eyes widen, and I spin around in shame, but the sudden movement causes my stomach to roll, and I feel like I'm going to be sick. Putting one foot in front of the other, I race back into the room I woke up in and make it to the toilet just in time. I throw up and once my throat has opened, everything in my body decides it wants out, and I vomit like that kid in *The Exorcist.*

"Ugh," I groan into the bowl when I finally stop, and then I jolt in fright when I feel a wet washcloth land on my neck.

Looking over my shoulder, I see Jett standing there. Concern is etched on his face but before I can say anything, another wave of nausea hits, and I vomit once again. "Ugh, I'm never drinking again."

"I call lies," Jett says from behind me. I can't help but chuckle because if I had a dollar for every time I said that statement, I'd be a very rich lady. "Can I get you anything, Margot?"

"My dignity back," I voice into the toilet. "This is so embarrassing."

"Babe, we've all vomited after a big night before."

"Yeah, but we aren't even friends."

"Ohh, well, I kinda thought we were."

My head snaps up and I look at him. "I, ummm, pucking hell."

"Did you just say pucking hell?"

"Yeah, I did, but I think in this state fuck me dead is a more appropriate statement." He laughs. "This is no laughing matter, Jensen. I feel like death and you're teasing me."

"I'm not teasing and from where I'm standing, it's extremely funny."

"Fuck you," I mutter.

"Look at you using real swears."

Somehow, I manage to flip him the bird, and this causes him to chuckle harder, and I find myself grinning up at the man before me.

"Is this my punishment for drinking too many margaritas last night?" The question is more to myself but before he can answer, I vomit, again.

And again.

And again.

"Did you eat last night?" he asks, taking the cloth from my nape and rinsing it before placing it back on my neck.

"Eating is cheating," I tell him.

"You are too cute," he says. His words float over my body and make me feel less crappy in this moment, but then my stomach gurgles and that less crappy feeling dissipates. "Ugh, I don't feel cute right now."

"You're always cute ... especially when you have vomit on your chin and in your hair."

Flipping him the bird, I quickly wipe at my chin, and when my hand comes back clean, I snap my gaze back to a quietly giggling-like-a-schoolgirl Jett.

"Here, drink this," he says and hands me a glass of water.

Before I can make things worse—not sure that's possible right now but this is me we are talking about —I grab the glass and take a sip. Swishing the water around in my mouth, I turn and spit into the toilet. Turning back, I smile up at him, but before I get to tell him he's a jerkface for teasing a hungover woman and thank him for looking after said hungover woman, I power vomit all over Jett's sweatpants.

My eyes widen and the embarrassment I already felt increases tenfold. "Ohhh, fuck," I hiss. Pulling my legs up, I cover my face in embarrassment. Tears well in my eyes, and when I lift my gaze to Jett's, his face is etched with shock, and the first tear falls. This is more embarrassing than the time I tripped on the subway and flashed my hoo-ha to a bunch of priests. "I'm so fucking sorry, Jett."

"Nothing to apologize for," he says, placating me.

"How can you say that? I just vomited all over you."

"It's a little bit of vomit on my sweats. It's fine. Now, can I get you anything?"

"A time machine to go back in time and not drink so much and then I won't vomit on you."

"That I cannot do, but I can whip you up some eggs, or I can make you Anton's—"

"Yes!" I shout at him. Anton Seaton, the captain of the Crushers has the best hangover cure in the whole entire universe, and it's the one and only time I ever eat, well drink, kale.

"Grab a shower and I'll whip you up one of his smoothies."

"Thank you, Jett, I really appreciate it."

"Anytime." He turns to leave but before he does, he glances over his shoulder and stares down at me. He's really concerned and that look on his face right now does something to me ... in that it causes me to vomit again. But vomit aside, I feel like we had a silent moment, and I don't know what to make of that.

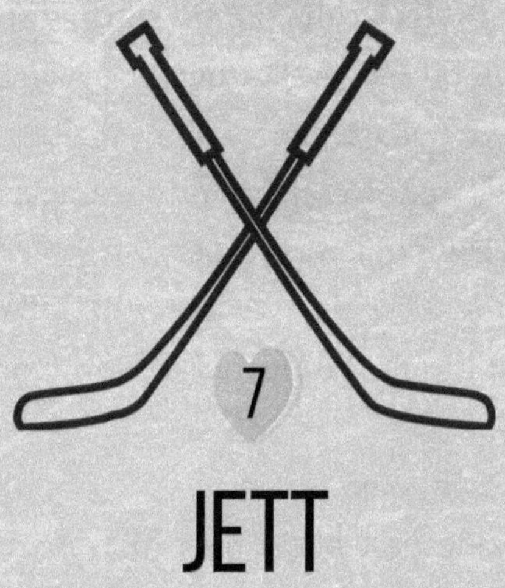

JETT

Leaving an embarrassed Margot in the bathroom, I head into the kitchen to make her a smoothie, but before I do that, I need to change my sweats. Walking to the laundry room, I kick them off and bend down to pick up a clean pair from the laundry basket.

"Jett," a soft voice calls out, and when I turn around, I come face-to-face with Margot. Her eyes widen when she notices I'm naked. "Holy shit," she gasps, "you're naked." Her gaze roams down my body and when her eyes land on my dick, they widen. "You're huge ... and it's beautiful." She covers her mouth when she realizes what she said. I don't want her to feel any more embarrassment so I quickly pull on my sweats, but I can't help the grin on my face at her assessment of my dick.

"What's up?" I nonchalantly ask as if she didn't just see, or compliment, my dick.

"I ... umm." Her eyes are still locked on my crotch, and I grin. "Wondered if I can ummm, ahhh, get a towel?"

"Ohh yeah, sure."

Squeezing past her, I open the linen cupboard and hand her a towel.

"Holy shit, this is so soft," she tells me as she caresses the towel in her hands.

"Right? My sister has good taste in linens."

"Guessing she's also responsible for the super soft sheets you have on your bed too?"

"You'd guess correctly."

A silence envelops us, but before it becomes awkward, she turns on her heels and heads into my room to have a shower ... then I start thinking of her naked. The water cascading down her body, but I quickly chase that thought away. We're friends, nothing more.

With thoughts of a wet and naked Margot pushed aside—sort of—I head into the kitchen and get to work on her hangover smoothie. As I blend it all together, thoughts of a wet and naked Margot pop back into my head and I realize, as she would say, I'm pucked when it comes to this woman.

8

MARGOT

"Thanks for the smoothie, but I, umm, think I should go," I say after I've had my drink and a piece of toast. I feel somewhat human again, but I think I've overstayed my welcome. Hell, I threw up on the guy and he still wants me around.

Jett Jensen is amazing, plain and simple.

"You are more than welcome to stay," he offers, and as much as I want to say yes, I need to get home.

"Thanks, but I need to get ready for the week ahead ... and don't you have practice?"

He looks to the clock on the wall. "Shit," he hisses. "I'm gonna be late and Coach is gonna kick my ass."

"You go and I'll clean this up," I offer.

"Are you sure?"

"It's the least I can do since you looked after me and then I vomited on you."

"You're the best." With that, he kisses me on my cheek, grabs his things, and hightails it out of here.

Coach Maxwell, aka my second dad, is a hard-ass. I've seen him push the guys to their limits, and you don't want to piss him off ... just ask Douche-man. But that douche deserved everything thrown his douchey way.

Pushing those thoughts aside, I clean up Jett's kitchen and throw in a load of laundry too.

Once his apartment is all sparkly and his clothes are washed and in the dryer, I head home to repeat what I just did ... minus the vomiting.

When my place is clean, I drop down onto the sofa and watch a rerun of *Friends*. I drift off to sleep and start dreaming ...

... I'm standing in the middle of the room wearing my favorite halter dress. My heels hurt my feet like a bitch, but they make my legs look amazing so I suck it up and look fabulous.

A hand slides around my waist, and I lean back

into a muscular chest. A hard shaft presses into my ass so I wriggle my hips.

"You keep that up," a deep voice whispers, "and I'm going to take you into the other room and fuck you."

Glancing over my shoulder, I lick my lips. "That's not a punishment."

Before I take my next breath, I'm being dragged into said other room. Once inside, he pushes me into the wall and covers my mouth with his. His tongue plunges in and out of my mouth. He slides his knee between my legs, and unabashedly, I begin to grind myself on him.

"Please," I beg into his mouth.

He drops to his knees and lifts my dress up. "No panties?" he growls, his heated breath causes my skin to tingle and my pussy to drip.

"You know I never wear them—"

"VPL," we both say at the same time, and then he licks up my slit, and I moan like a wanton hussy.

"Yes," I mewl, "fuck me with your tongue."

"Shhh," he commands, "or you'll have to wait till later."

Nodding, I comply as he begins to feast on me. Suddenly, my body tightens.

The fuse is lit.

Then I explode.

I come hard and cry out his name as I do, "Jett."

My eyes fly open and I lie here, breathing deeply with a throbbing between my thighs. Bringing my hand to my chest, I rest it over my heart and begin to steady my breathing as I come back down to Earth. I've never orgasmed in a dream before, but fuck me sideways, that was hot. Dream Jett really knows how to work a girl over. My vagina is still pulsing, but it all stops abruptly when I remember who I dream-gasmed over.

Grabbing my phone, I shoot off a text. I need reinforcements and I need them now.

MARGOT

I need you.

Stat

Bring tequila

Actually, just tea … I'm never drinking again

Dropping my phone onto the sofa next to me, I wait for my bestie to get back to me. There's a knock at my door less than an hour later and I smile. My bestie is an uber bestie and came running in my time of need. "I love you, Chels," I mumble as I roll off my couch and shuffle to my door, but when I open it, I'm surprised at who my visitor is.

"Jett, what are you doing here?" I ask, my voice laced with shock.

"I wanted to make sure you were okay."

"I'm fine, just hungover." *And coming down from a dream of you tongue fucking me like I've never been tongue fucked before.* As I stare at the leading man in my dream just now, I realize I'm pucked when it comes to Jett Jensen.

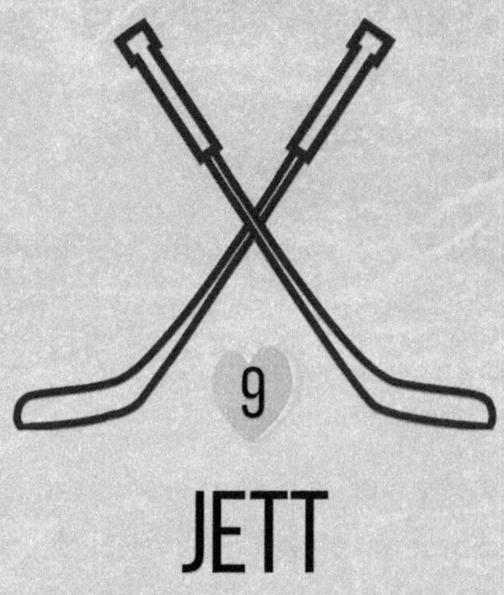

JETT

"I wanted to make sure you were okay." My eyes roam over her and I notice she's flushed and a little sweaty. "You're a little flushed and sweating. Are you sure you aren't getting sick?"

"No no," I protest, "I'm fine, just hungover."

Nodding, I purse my lips, but I don't believe her one iota. "Do you need me to get you anything?"

"I'm fine, really," she tries to reassure me. "Do you, ummm, ahh, wanna come in?"

"Yeah, okay," I agree with a nod.

She steps aside and ushers me in. Glancing around, I smile as I take in her apartment. Due to the open layout, I can see the kitchen, dining nook, her bedroom, what I presume is the bathroom, and her living area. It's so Margot.

"Can I get you a drink?" she offers.

"Water, please."

She nods and heads over to the kitchen, and I follow. She hands me a bottle of water then she uncaps hers and takes a drink. I intently watch as she takes a sip.

"How was practice?" she asks before jumping up onto the counter, swinging her legs back and forth.

"Hard. Coach rode our asses today."

"That sounds like him." Silence envelops us but it's not awkward. She bites her lip. "Thanks again for last night ... and this morning."

"Don't mention it. I'm just glad you're okay."

"Anton's smoothie is a lifesaver."

"It sure is."

Another silence befalls us but her phone chimes with a text. She pulls it from her pocket and reads, furrowing her brow.

"Everything okay?"

"Yeah, just my boss. There's a charity dinner thing in a few weeks, and she's pushing me to bring a date since it's tables of ten and I'm the only single one. I was going to bring, Chels but she's busy and—"

"I'll go with you," I blurt out before thinking.

"Really?"

"Yeah, I'd love to go with you."

"You really wanna be my date?"

"Yep," I tell her again, letting the 'p' pop. "I've been told I rock a suit and I'm guessing there will be free food?"

"And a band."

"Then I'm sold."

"Thanks, Jett, I really appreciate it and if you ever need a date, I'm your girl. We can be each other's fake date."

Getting all the details about the event, I add it to my calendar, say my goodbyes, and head off. On the way out, I pass Chelsea on the stairs. She looks at me questioningly, but we don't stop to chat. Chelsea and I don't have a relationship like that.

Hailing a cab, I jump in and head home. Just as I arrive at my place, my sister messages me.

> **SADIE**
>
> Got a date yet?

> **JETT**
>
> I don't need one

> **SADIE**
>
> Two words, Lisa/Adam Caldwell

What is with the women in my life wanting me

to settle down? My mind drifts to Margot, and I find myself smiling, she's the type of woman I want to settle down with. Maybe I'll ask her to be my fake date. With that plan in my mind, to get my sister off my back, I give her a bone.

JETT

That was three

SADIE

Jett Jensen ….

JETT

Okay, fine, I might have a date

SADIE

Did you meet someone?

JETT

No

Maybe, but I can't tell my sister that. I don't even know what it is I feel for Margot. But ever since this morning, I haven't been able to stop thinking about her.

SADIE

Does my baby bro have a secret girlfriend?

JETT

I have a friend who is a girl

SADIE

But you want her more than just a
girl space friend? You want her as a
GIRLfriend, one word

JETT

No ... maybe ... I don't know

As soon as I reread my last message, I follow it up with a quick.

JETT

Please don't call me about this ...
or tell Mom. I'm about to crash. I
have early practice.

Not a total lie because I do have practice, but I know my sister. She'll want to know all the details about Margot, and I don't know any details. All I know is, right now, I can't stop thinking about her, but we're just friends.

SADIE

Fine

Her response shocks me but when another message comes through immediately after, I roll my eyes as I read.

SADIE

Just name your firstborn after me

JETT

Nite Sadie

SADIE

Nite Jett

With my sister placated, for now, I throw my phone onto the side table. Then I strip off and hop into the shower. Once I'm washed and dried, I climb naked into bed and snuggle under the covers.

My pillows still smell like Margot, and for some reason, I don't ever want to wash them again. Margot has overtaken my thoughts and my bed, what's up with that?

10
MARGOT

... a few weeks later

"Ugh," I groan and when I look around, I shake my head. I need to stop waking up hungover in Jett's bed, people are going to start talking. Even though we are nothing, just two friends who go out together, one of them always ends up looking after the other because one—me—doesn't know how to say no to Slade and his killer—literally—margaritas or beer.

The last few weeks have seen the two of us accompanying each other to several events together so we aren't the loser single people.

Last night was my charity work thing. I may have

indulged in too much champagne ... and I think I bought something to do with golf in the charity auction.

Like every time I sleep over, I wake up in one of Jett's shirts and my hair looks like two birds went to a rave. Thankfully this morning, I don't feel like vomiting—fist pump—probably because I was drinking the good bubbly last night and not the two-for-one crap I usually drink, but my head is pounding. I need water and Anton's smoothie, stat.

Climbing out of bed, I make my way out of his bedroom. Shuffling my feet along the soft beige carpet, I stop in the hallway when I hear two voices coming from the living area.

"I need to know your date's name, Jett."

"And I told you, I don't need a date."

"And I told you, Mom is going to set you up with Lisa, or Adam, Caldwell if you don't bring someone, and you and I both know a brick wall would be more fun to hang out with than either of them, so just give me a freakin' name."

"I ..."

Before my brain catches up to my mouth, I enter the room. "Her name is Margot."

11

JETT

Hearing those four words has both my sister and I turning toward the sound of the voice. The voice that floats over my body and causes my blood to zing within my veins.

"Who the hell are you?" Sadie growls. Protective sister mode has been activated.

"Margot," we both say at the same time.

"Well then, Margot, what are you doing here?"

"Umm, I ..."

She stammers and it's the first time I've ever seen her rattled. "She stayed here last night," I inform my sister, walking over to Margot, apologizing with my eyes for my sister's behavior.

"Is she your girlfriend?" Sadie questions.

Now it's my turn to hesitate, "Umm ..."

While Margot replies with a stern, "We don't have to define our relationship to you."

"Excuse me?" my sister hisses, shocked that someone would talk to her like that. "Just who do you think you are, speaking to me like that?"

"Who I am is no concern of yours, but for what it's worth, I'm Margot Radclyff and I'm a Virgo. I like beer and margaritas. I'm into reading smutty books and I'm not ashamed of that. I'm a graphic designer by day and a kick-ass karaoke queen on the weekends."

"That still doesn't explain why you're here."

"Well, la—"

"Margot," I interrupt her, "can you give me and my sister a moment?"

"Sure," she says, then Margot looks to Sadie and smiles. "It was nice meeting you." Without another word, she turns around and heads back into my bedroom.

"What the hell, Jett? Who is that woman? And why is she in your jersey with bed hair?"

"She umm, I ... fuck."

"Is she a puck bunny?"

"No," I snap, "she's not a bunny, and don't ever refer to her as one again."

"Okay. Okay." She raises her hands in defeat. "Who is she?"

"She's a friend."

My sister's eyes widen, and I know she's thinking about the text I sent her a few weeks back about my girl space friend.

"You and I can discuss your *girl* friend," she air quotes girl, "at a later time." Sadie's gaze flicks from the hallway to me and back several times. I'm waiting for the 'Sadie interrogation' to begin but shocking me, she just smiles, stands up, and begins to gather her things. "I'm gonna go and leave you and your girl space friend to do whatever it is you were going to do today." She places her coffee mug in the sink and spins to face me. "Just remember, if it's not on, it's not on."

"Sadie," I admonish her and shake my head.

"I'm just looking out for my bro. As much as I'd rock being an aunty, hold off 'cause I wanna give Momma a grandbaby before you."

"Deal," I tell her.

"And I'll put Margot down as your plus one." She walks over to me and leans down to kiss me on the cheek. Then she whispers, "And for the record, I'm glad you've found someone. She seems like a ballbuster and just what you need."

Without another word, she exits my apartment and leaves me sitting here miffed at her parting words. I stare at the closed door, wondering what the hell just happened.

"Is the coast clear?" a soft voice says from behind me. Turning around, my eyes land on Margot's, and I notice she's dressed in her outfit from last night.

"Sorry about that, my sister is ..."

"Protective of her brother and worried that I'm some puck bunny who's trying to get my grubby mitts into you."

"Pretty much," I confirm.

"So, what's this event I'm now attending with you?"

"You really don't have to do that."

"I know, but it seems like you need someone to go with you and I'm a girl. I like dressing up and I like free food. It's a win-win for me when you think about it."

"You really want to be my fake date to my sister's wedding to stave off my mother and her horrible matchmaking abilities?"

She nods. "I'd love to be your fake date, Jett."

Her words warm my heart, and I smile over at my friend. And that's what Margot and I are, we're friends who help each other but why, just now, did my heart stutter at the word fake?

12
MARGOT

"Wʜᴀᴛ's ᴡɪᴛʜ ʏᴏᴜ ᴀɴᴅ Jᴇᴛᴛ?" Cʜᴇʟsᴇᴀ ᴀsᴋs while the guys are at the bar getting another round of drinks. They played the Vancouver Vikings earlier and lost 3-2. The mood tonight in Squires is somber, but Chels and I are on a mission to cheer the team up. And I'm sure when I get up and start karaoke, they will be smiling and cheering for me ... to get off the stage. I cannot sing for my life, but I love getting up on that stage and belting out "Wannabe" by the Spice Girls.

"Nothing," I refute but my volume increases. My bestie knows I'm full of shit and she gives me the eye. "We just help each other out from time to time. It's pucking fake."

"Yeah, and Doucheman is a saint," she throws back at me.

"Saint Asshat," I reply.

Stefan Däuchmen is Chelsea's douchey ex. He certainly lives up to his däuchy last name, well not of late, but he'll always be a douche. Thankfully he lives in LA now and is out of our lives, well, except for when the Crushers play, and smash, the LA Legends on the ice.

"You and I both know he's not a total douche."

"Are we in the *Twilight Zone?* You're defending him."

"No, we are not in the *Twilight Zone,* but I've seen a change in him since Wren has been working with him. Occasionally, I see the Stefan I fell in love with. I don't want to see his life implode." Now it's my turn to give her the eye because he really fucked my bestie over. "Don't give me that look, Margot. You know I'm right, and if I'm not mistaken, at one point in time, you were friends with the guy too."

"He lost my friendship when he fucked all those bunnies in your bed and apartment. No one hurts my friend."

"And while I appreciate your unwavering support, I've forgiven him. Life is too short to hold grudges and it's too short to fake things ... even though deep down you know it should be more than fake."

"You need to lay off the beers, Chels."

"I will drink what I want to drink, and I will forgive who I want to forgive. Now, forget about Doucheman and tell me why you won't accept that this thing with Jett is more than just fake?"

"Because it's just fake."

She opens her mouth to say more, but the guys return with pitchers of beer and a tray of shots. Looks like the commiserating of the loss is stepping up.

Jett pours beers for everyone and when he passes me mine, he smiles and I find myself smiling back at him. He winks and then pours another and the moment is gone.

The rest of the night is filled with beers, shots, laughs, and karaoke. Lots of karaoke.

Jett and I even do a duet, singing "(I've Had) The Time of My Life" by Bill Medley and Jennifer Warnes, and I seriously am having the time of my life.

As we wait for a cab at stupid a.m., I lean on Jett for support. He slides his arm around my waist, and when I lift my gaze up to him, I wonder if we could be more. *Damn you, Chelsea, planting ideas in my head.*

13

JETT

It's been a roller coaster of a few weeks. What with Christmas and New Year's and a string of away games. JJ and Lexi finally got their shit together and are a couple. Then, last week, the team was rocked by the loss of Rachelle McQueen, the wife of our assistant coach, Rick. She died while giving birth to their fourth child and today is her funeral.

As much as it's been tough, I'm thankful to have had Margot by my side. The two of us talk almost every day, and when I'm away, we either FaceTime or text. She's also stepped in several times and been my 'girlfriend' when we've been out and things with a bunny have gotten too intense. Like my sister said, she's a real ballbuster but also fun, flirty, and perfect.

She's become a really good friend of mine and I'm thankful to have her in my life.

"What's up with you and Margot?" Kallen asks, dropping into the seat next to me in Rick's house.

"What do you mean?" I ask, feigning ignorance, but I know what he's alluding to. It's the same question ALL my teammates have been asking me lately.

"You and Margot, you two are mighty cozy when you're together." He waggles his eyebrows at me and I'm not sure if he's having a stroke or if he's alluding to something sexual happening between Margot and me.

"We're just helping each other out. It's all pucking fake."

I'm met with silence. When I turn my head to him, he has a look on his face that tells me he thinks I'm full of shit, and I have a feeling he's right. The more time I spend with her, the more I like her.

"You keep telling yourself that, Jett, but the spark between you two is electric and if I can see it, everyone else can too."

Turning away from him, I look across the room and take a moment to stare at her. Margot is gorgeous, there's no other way to describe her. She's funny and outgoing. She's the perfect woman. Kallen's words percolate in my brain. Maybe I need to explore this with her, but whatever I decide, it will have to wait because today isn't about me and my dick. Today is about paying respect to Rachelle McQueen and being here for our assistant coach and his family.

As the day progresses, I find myself looking for Margot more than I should be. She's currently in the living room playing cards with Cate, Rick's youngest daughter.

"Just go for it," a deep voice says from behind me, and when I turn around, I come face-to-face with Rick.

"I don't know what you're talking about, Coach McQueen."

"You're not supposed to lie to a man who's grieving. You're supposed to listen to his wise advice."

"And what advice do you have for me, Coach?"

"Life's too short to fake it, Jensen. Don't waste a moment. Don't second-guess. Take her by the cheeks, look into her eyes, and tell her you love her. Tell her she means everything to you and you love her more than hockey." He swallows deeply. "Or something like that. Don't take chances when it comes to love because fate is a pucking bitch. She takes what she wants. Don't live with regrets. Live with love in your heart."

Before I can reply, he walks away and scoops up his new baby, Cameron. He kisses his son's head and whispers, "We love you, baby boy."

How can the most joyous of occasions be fraught with such tragedy?

My gaze once again lands on Margot, and when she sadly smiles at me, I make the decision to find out where she stands. Coach McQueen is right, life is too short to fake it.

14
MARGOT

IT'S THE DAY OF LOVE AND I'M OFF TO JETT'S sister's wedding as his fake date. It feels weird celebrating love when one of the most amazing couples I know has just been torn apart. Game days will not be the same without Rachelle's bright and bubbly persona infecting everyone around her.

Putting thoughts of Rachelle aside, I slip into my navy-blue satin halter dress. It shows just a hint of cleavage but there's a killer slit in the side, which showcases my legs. I pair it with heels that accentuate said legs.

Jett seems nervous about today, turns out his

mom is super excited to meet me, the *girlfriend*. She's over the moon her baby boy has met someone. I kinda feel bad that we're deceiving her. Personally, I think she should be focusing on her daughter since it's her wedding, but what do I know, I'm not a mom.

There's a knock at my door. "Coming," I shout out as I recap my mascara.

Racing over to the door, I swing it open, and my eyes widen when I see Jett. He's wearing black slacks that I'm sure showcase his delectable ass. His shirt is the same color as my dress and the top few buttons are undone. "You scrub up good, Jensen."

"As do you, Radclyff. Give me a spin."

With a nonchalant shrug, I spin on my heel, but I spin a little too quickly and lose my balance. Luckily for me, Jett and his quick reflexes catch me. His arms slide around my waist, and I grip his shoulders.

Our eyes lock.

Neither one of us moves.

We stare at one another intently, my eyes drop to his lips and when his tongue darts out, I suddenly want to kiss him.

Our heads gravitate toward one another and then his lips are on mine.

Jett

Jensen

Is

Kissing

Me.

The kiss starts out soft and then it's anything but. Our tongues slip and slide in each other's mouths. You can't tell where Jett ends and I start.

Fuck me sideways, Cupid, this kiss is everything.

All too soon, Jett lifts me back upright and we breathlessly pull apart. Lifting my hand, I cover my mouth. Never before have my lips tingled like this after a kiss.

"I, just, umm, need to finish getting ready."

"You are perfectly perfect, Margot Radclyff."

A smile appears on my face. "That's the nicest compliment I have ever received but I need lipstick to complete my outfit. Give me a minute." Before he can reply, I spin—without falling this time—and head into the bathroom to apply my lipstick ... and take a few moments to calm my racing heart. I want more kisses like that, but it's only fake. We were clearly caught up in the moment but as I swipe on my pale pink lipstick, I mentally plan how I turn fake to real.

JETT

Tonight has not started off how I expected it to. It's certainly off with a bang and we haven't even arrived at the wedding yet as fake dates. For the last week, I have reiterated to my sister that nothing is happening between Margot and me ... even though Coach McQueen's words of '*Life's too short to fake it, Jensen. Don't waste a moment,*' have played on repeat.

And that kiss just now makes me think maybe there is something there between us because that kiss is a kiss for the history books.

Now, as I stand here and watch her walk into her bathroom to finish getting ready, I'm even more confused.

Walking farther into Margot's apartment, I drop down onto her sofa to wait for her. My mind drifts back to that kiss. It was so much better than any kiss I have ever had before.

Maybe I need to take a chance and explore this.

Margot and I have a blast when we're together. Our friends get along well and I know she's not a bunny after my money or the fame that comes from being with an NHL player.

When she walks back out, my eyes land on her lips and I want to feel them against mine again, but we need to get going. Me and my fake love life will need to wait.

The ceremony is beautiful, and love is all around us as we walk from the garden over to the reception on the outdoor terrace. Sadie and Ricky look happy, and I find myself smiling as I make my way over to the happy couple.

"Congrats, man," I say to Ricky, offering him my hand when I reach them. "And, Sade, you look beautiful."

"Thanks, Jett." Then she ignores me and looks to Margot at my side. "Thanks for coming, Margot."

"Thanks for having me, and congratulations. It was a beautiful ceremony."

"It was, wasn't it?" my sister replies, and it's not in a cocky way. It's in that 'thank fuck it all worked out' kind of way. "You'll be next," my sister teases.

Margot's eyes widen and I just shake my head.

"Let's get a drink," I say, and Margot nods. Offering her my hand, she slides hers into mine and we make our way over to the bar.

"Two champagnes, please," I ask the bartender.

"Holy shit, you're Jett Jensen. Left-wing for the New York Crushers," he says. His face lights up like the Jumbotron on game day.

"I sure am."

"You're my favorite player."

"Thanks, man, I appreciate it, but today is about my sister."

"Ohh, yeah, sure but do you, umm, think I can get a pic and an autograph?"

"Sure," I tell him, "but first, can you get my date a drink?"

"I'm happy to wait," Margot refutes with a shake of her head, just as the bartender says, "Yeah, sure."

He pours a drink for Margot and then hands me

a napkin and a pen. I quickly sign it for him while he comes around the bar for our pic together.

"Thanks, man, you just made my year."

He slides back behind the bar and pours me a drink. Taking Margot's hand, I walk us over to where my parents are standing. "Mom. Dad, this is Margot," I say when we reach them, "Margot, this is my mom and dad."

"Hi, Mr. and Mrs. Jensen," she timidly says with a finger wave.

"Please," Dad admonishes her, "call us Ray and Sara. Mr. Jensen was my dad and he was an asshole."

"Ray," Mom scolds him and slaps Dad on the arm. "He's pulling your leg, dear, Papa Jensen was—God rest his soul—a total sweetheart and wouldn't hurt a fly. Much like my Jett here."

Margot chuckles. "He sounds like my nanna. She's a total sweetheart, but you mess with her or those she loves and it's game on."

"So you take after her?" I ask.

"If I'm half as amazing as Nanna Radclyff, then I'll be living my best life."

"Well, you are kind, tenacious, and a ballbuster, Sadie's exact words. You have this aurora that sucks people in, and they are better off for knowing you."

Her gaze is locked on mine and she smiles at my

words. That little lip lift has my heart stuttering in my chest.

"Dance with me?" I blurt out.

She looks to the dance floor off to the side and then back to me. "Ummm, Jett, no one is dancing."

Silence envelops the four of us but it's not awkward. It's broken when Dad looks to Mom. "Let's dance."

"I'd love to," Mom coos with hearts in her eyes.

Dad looks to Margot. "They are now."

And then he pulls Mom out onto the dance floor. Sadie and Rickey join them as do several of the other guests.

Looking back to my gorgeous date, I waggle my eyebrows and nod to the dance floor. "What do you say, Radclyff? Wanna dance with me?"

16
MARGOT

How can one simple question cause my heart to flutter like it is right now?

Jett and I have danced before, but this, this feels different.

My head starts nodding of its own accord and then he offers me his hand. Placing mine in his, a spark jolts between us when our palms touch. When he laces our fingers together, an inferno wraps itself around us.

Jett escorts us into the middle of the dance floor. He spins me out and tugs me back in. In a suave James Bondesque move, his hand effortlessly slides around my waist. It rests precariously low on my back and then he pulls me closer to him.

Our bodies begin to move to the music and even though we're in the middle of the dance floor, everyone around us fades into the background. It's just Jett and I dancing under the fairy lights.

It's perfect in every way.

Closing my eyes, I rest my head on Jett's shoulder and let the music wrap itself around us, but our perfect moment is broken when dinner is announced. We all shuffle off the dance floor and find our seats.

Jett, ever the gentleman, pulls my chair out for me. Before he takes his seat, he presses a kiss to my temple and my body melts at the gesture. Lifting my head, I stare up at him. His eyes are locked on mine, and I feel his gaze deep within my soul.

"Come with me," he commands, and before I know what's happening, I'm rising out of my chair before Jett and I race back out to the outdoor area.

Like on the dance floor earlier, he slides his hands around my hips and pulls me into him. My hands land on his chest and my eyes, once again, are locked on his.

"Kiss me, Margot," he growls. The deep timbre of his voice vibrates around me. It's a request, not a question. I stand here, at his sister's wedding reception, and mutely stare up at him.

For the first time in my life, I'm speechless.

"What?" I murmur.

"I said kiss me," he repeats. He lifts his hand, cups my cheek, and runs the pad of his thumb over my lips. "Press those beautiful lips against mine and kiss me."

Before I know what's happening, my body leans the last few millimeters into him and I press my lips tentatively to his. As soon as our lips touch, like earlier in my apartment, a fuse is lit and it's a flurry of activity.

Every nerve ending in my body comes alive when he pushes his tongue into my mouth, and like the wanton hussy I am, I suck and kiss him back.

In the background, Ed sings about kissing and falling in love as the two of us continue to kiss passionately.

Pulling back from another kiss of all kisses, he rests his forehead against mine. "I know this is just fake, Margot, but I want you. I need you. Please, please give me a chance to love you ... for real."

17

JETT

"... I want you. I need you. Please, please give me a chance to love you ... for real."

Our hurried breaths mingle together as she processes my words. "Jett, I, this ..."

She steps back from me, and my heart shatters within my chest.

Have I read this all wrong? Is she just caught up in the day of love and my sister's wedding? But then she utters two words that change everything.

"Fuck it," spills from her lips and then she throws herself at me.

Catching her, she wraps her arms around my neck and our lips collide in a heated and frenzied kiss. Our tongues tangle. They plunge in and out of each other's mouths, erotically sliding around together.

"I want you," she whispers against my lips as she presses her body into mine. If there weren't sixty people just a few feet away inside, I'd lay her down on the outdoor deck and fuck her senseless.

"I want you, too, but we're at my sister's wedding and dinner is about to be served."

"Luckily for you, I like food and free booze but later, it's game on."

"Deal," I reply, a megawatt grin on my face. "Besides, if these kisses are anything to go by, we're going to need sustenance for the night ahead. But, Margot, just know, as soon as we leave here, don't expect to leave my bed until I've fucked you six ways to Sunday."

"Game on," she sassily says.

Slamming my lips to hers again, I slide my arms around her waist and kiss her with everything I have. After only a few kisses, I'm pucked when it comes to this woman. Now that I have her, I'm never letting her go.

We head back inside just as the starter is served to our table. No one questions what we were up to, but from Margot's flushed cheeks, people know.

My phone pings with a text and I slide it out.

When I see Sadie's name on the screen, I furrow my brows and snap my eyes to her sitting at the head table next to her new husband. She eyes my phone so I turn my attention back to it.

SADIE

Did you just fuck Margot at my wedding?

JETT

A gentleman never tells

But for the record, no, I did not. I have more respect for you than to do that

SADIE

Respect schmespect, fuck her.

JETT

Are you pimping me out at your wedding?

SADIE

If it means you get laid, then yes, call me Pimp Diddy Sadie

A snort slips out at her 'Pimp Diddy Sadie' comment, causing those around me to look at me inquisitively, including the beauty sitting next to me.

JETT

Stop focusing on me and focus on your husband … you know, the guy you just promised to love and cherish forever

Maybe you two need to fuck???

SADIE

Who says we haven't??? **wink wink**

But seriously, you deserve to be happy, Jetster. I've never seen you light up around a woman like this before. Don't fuck it up with Margot … I like her

JETT

I like her too

SADIE

Then DON'T FUCK IT UP!!!!!!

Sliding my phone back into my pocket, I look at the woman next to me and hope with everything I have that I don't fuck it up. She's amazing and I want to see where this goes.

18
MARGOT

The rest of the wedding flies by quickly. Jett and I dance, we laugh … we kiss. Boy, oh boy, do we kiss, and then by some twisted twist of fate, I catch the bouquet.

"Ohhhh, you're next, big bro," Sadie sings out to her brother in a teasing tone, causing everyone, me included, to laugh.

She waltzes over to me and pulls me into a hug. "I'm happy you two finally got your shit together," she murmurs into my ear. Pulling back, I look inquisitively at her. "I knew from the morning I first met you that you two would end up together."

"How?" I ask, completely confused. *My feelings for Jett weren't there then*, I think, but subconsciously, deep down, I was already falling for Jett. That sexy dream I had kinda gave away what I was really feeling. After all, they say your dreams are the eyes to your deepest desires or some crap like that ... maybe, I don't know, I'm not a dream expert.

"The way he looks at you," she says, and we both look toward the man in question. He's staring at us, well me. "He only has eyes for you, Margot. He defended you when I called you a bunny AND the kicker, he invited you to a family event. He's never, and I mean never, ever, ever brought anyone home before." My eyes widen at that revelation.

"Bullshit," I scoff.

"I shit you not," she replies. "Trust me, if he wasn't interested, he would have let Mom set him up with Lisa or Adam tonight."

Without uttering another word, she spins on her heel and walks over to her husband. He pulls her into him and kisses her, everyone around them cheers and hollers, and someone—Jett—yells, "Get a room."

"So, seems you're next," Jett says when he finally re-joins me.

"Seems so ... you know anyone who wants to get hitched?" He waggles his eyebrows. "Settle down, hockey stud. A few amazing kisses do not equal marriage."

He leans over and presses a quick kiss to my lips. "How many kisses will it take?" he flirtily says.

Smiling at him, I nonchalantly reply with a shrug.

"Tell me," he demands. "How many will it take?"

"A lifetime's worth of kisses."

"That can be arranged," he matter-of-factly tells me. "Wanna get out of here?"

"Isn't it customary for the bride and groom to leave first?"

"Probably, but I've been thinking about stripping this sexy dress off your gorgeous body and kissing you from head to toe before I sink my cock into you and you forget your name, all fucking night."

"Jett Jensen," I playfully scoff, "who knew you had such a dirty mouth?"

"There's a lot you don't know about me."

"Like what?"

"For starters, I think you're the most beautiful woman in the world. Now that I have my chance with you, I'm gonna pull out all the stops because as I said earlier, Margot, you are perfectly perfect ... for me."

Staring at him, my heart is full and my vagina is

throbbing and leaking. This man is not who I thought he was, he's everything I thought ... and more.

As I stand here, holding the bouquet beside the man who has weaseled his way into my heart, I realize that for the first time ever, I want a relationship. I want it all with him. No longer are we fake, we're something beautiful and it's just the beginning. Smiling brightly, I outstretch my hand. "Let's get out of here."

JETT

As soon as the door to my apartment clicks closed, it's game on.

Spinning Margot around, I push her up against the wall and cover her mouth with mine. Grabbing her hands, I lift her arms over her head and hold them there. My other hand skates down her arm, across her collarbone, and to her chest. Circling her nipple, I cup her boob and continue my downward path over her stomach before I cup her pussy through her dress. Her heat warms my palm as I press it into her. She moans into my mouth and it's music to my ears ... and dick.

"Please," she mumbles into our kiss.

Pulling back, I stare at her flushed face. "Please what?"

"Just please," she begs, and who am I to deny her.

Dropping to my knees, I lift the hem of her dress and bunch the material at her waist. Leaning forward, I lick up her trembling thigh and nuzzle her clit with my nose. Poking my tongue out, I push it into her panty-covered slit and suck.

"Yes," she mewls.

Pushing the material aside, I get a look at her pussy but it's not enough. "Hope you aren't attached to these," I voice, and before she can answer, I pull at the material and rip her panties from her body. Bringing the shredded material to my nose, I inhale. She smells delicious and I cannot wait to get a taste.

Dropping her shredded panties to the tiles, I look at her bare mound and smile when I see it's hair free, except for a heart-shaped landing strip. "Is that a love heart?"

"Mmmhmpf," she replies with a nod.

"I love it," I tell her. Then I shove my face into her mound. I lick and suck and fuck her with my tongue.

"More," she demands.

So I give her more. I slide a finger into her hole and hook it, pressing on that pressure point, which causes her to explode. Her juices coat my face, and she babbles incoherently as she rides through her release.

Her body relaxes and I pull my finger from her. Bringing it to my mouth, I suck. Never have I tasted anything so delicious. "Exquisite," I tell her.

"That ... was ... ah-may-zing," she pants.

"You ain't seen nothing yet, baby."

20
MARGOT

HOLY SHIT, I INTERNALLY CHANT AS I STARE down at Jett. That was some orgasm. I don't think I've ever climaxed that hard from oral. Before I have a chance to catch my breath, Jett stands up and throws me over his shoulder. He marches through his apartment and into his bedroom. He places me back on my feet at the end of his bed and stares at me. "Strip," he orders.

I'm not usually a fan of the alpha bullshit, but right now, my hands cannot move fast enough to the clasp at the back of my neck. For the first time ever, the clasp opens easily. The silky material falls down my body, leaving me only in my heels since I went braless and Jett ripped my panties—literally ...

and it was totally hot by the way—off my body earlier.

"You are a vision, Margot."

My cheeks heat at the compliment. "Why thank you, but there seems to be one problem."

"What's that?"

"You have far too many clothes on."

"That I do, but give me a moment to appreciate you."

My cheeks darken further as his gaze roams over me. He starts by kicking off his shoes. Then he removes his jacket, dropping it to the carpet below. Next, he pulls his shirt free, and one by one, he pops open the buttons. Revealing muscle after glorious muscle. Hockey guys are ripped, and up close it's perfect ... perfectly perfect, as he would say.

Once his shirt is undone, he leaves it on and begins working on his pants as I trace my finger over his abs. Right now, it's like my very own *Magic Mike* show and I have front-row seats. He flips open the button and lowers his fly. Hooking his thumbs in the waistband, he removes both his pants and briefs in one fell swoop, leaving him naked except for his shirt.

"I want to see all of you," I tell him, "give me a little spin."

He nods and goes to remove his shirt. "No!" I shout. "Leave your shirt on."

With a nod, he spins around and lifts his shirt up. Giving me an up close and unobstructed view of his perfectly perfect ass. He finishes his circle and our gaze connects again.

"Your turn," he suggests.

Nodding, I spin around and when I'm facing him again, I push Lola and Lala together, circling my nipples with my index fingers.

"Mine," he growls. He pushes my hands away and cups my boobs in his palms. His hands dwarf my itty-bitty titties, but he doesn't seem to mind. He lowers his head and takes one of my nipples into his mouth and sucks. My head drops back and I let the sensation of his mouth on me take over.

"Get onto the bed," he growls, and like an obedient good girl, I crawl up the mattress. Climbing up to the pillows, I be sure to wiggle my ass in his face before I roll onto my back and spread my legs wide. Letting him see everything.

He licks his lips and lifts his hand to his dick and begins stroking.

"Like what you see?" I purr as I trace my finger down my chest, over my belly, and into my pussy. In and out I thrust my fingers, in time to his hand on his dick.

Pleasure builds with each flick of my wrist. I'm like a ticking time bomb, waiting for the moment of detonation. I need him and I need him now. "Please," I beg.

"Please what?"

"Please fuck me."

21

JETT

Best three words I have ever heard, and no sooner do they pass through her delectable lips am I climbing onto the bed. Like a tiger stalking its prey, I slide up her body, stopping to pay attention to her pussy. Placing a kiss on her mound, I kiss my way up her abdomen, kiss each breast, and then finally, I reach her lips.

My body cocoons hers as we make out.

She pushes up and grinds herself on me. "Fuck me, please," she demands again.

Reaching over, I dig in the drawer and pull out a foil packet. Sitting back on my haunches, I roll the condom down my shaft, giving it a few tugs before I lean forward and press the head between her folds.

We both hiss as I inch farther into her. When I'm fully seated, she lets out the sexiest sound and it increases as I begin to thrust my hips, driving my dick in and out of her.

We fall into a rhythm and I start to feel my balls tingle. I can't come until she does, so I increase my thrusts and slide my hand between us and begin rubbing her clit. It's what she needs and I feel her pussy clench my dick tighter. Then she's screaming my name as her orgasm spills free.

Seeing, hearing, and feeling her let loose causes me to join her. Together we tumble into the orgasmic bliss.

Rolling off her, I fall to my back and stare at the ceiling, each of us huffing and puffing.

"That," I pant, "was—"

"Perfectly perfect," she interrupts, and I smile at the phrase she used.

Turning my head, I stare and watch as she gets her breathing under control.

"Stop staring," she says. She rolls to her side and rests her head in the palm of her hand.

"I'm not staring, I'm admiring."

"Same-same, but for what it's worth, I like you staring at me."

"Good, 'cause I like staring at you."

"What else do you like?" she playfully asks, tracing her fingertip over my pec.

"Everything," I tell her. That one word holds so much meaning because I love everything about this woman, and I can see myself falling in love with her. Hell, I already *am* falling for her.

"Good, 'cause I love everything about you, too, Jett Jensen. Now, let's get some sleep, and if you play your cards right, you might wake up with my lips wrapped around your dick."

"Oooooor," I suggest, "we can have a nightcap where I drink your juices and you drink my cum."

"Are you proposing a sixty-nine, Mr. Jensen?"

"That I am, Ms. Radclyff."

"Well, then, you have yourself a deal."

"Excellent, now climb on my face and let me eat your pussy while you suck my dick."

And that's exactly what we do … and more.

21
EPILOGUE - JETT

"I now pronounce you, husband and wife," the minister says. My brother, David, grips his new wife's cheeks in his hands and kisses her. This was supposed to be their engagement party, but the two sneaky devils arranged a wedding. And like at my sister's wedding, Margot catches the bouquet.

My other brothers all turn to me and start humming, "The Wedding March," ... but what nobody knows is that tomorrow, I'm planning on proposing to Margot.

It's only been a couple of years since we officially started dating, but when you know, you know. From that first official fake date at her company's gala, I subconsciously knew she was the one.

She's my soul mate.

The peanut to my butter, and I now have a love just like my mom and dad's.

"That's two," Margot declares as she drops onto my lap, knocking me in the face with the bouquet.

"Ohhh, look at you, you can count."

She slaps me in the chest. "Hardy-har-har." And when she gazes into my eyes, something clicks. The need to propose slams into me so I decide to do it now. Lifting her into my arms, bridal style, I carry her across the room. Hoots and hollers—from my brothers—follow us but I ignore them all.

I'm a man on a mission and nothing is going to stop me.

Stepping outside, I walk across the garden and down a pathway to the beach. Coming to the water's edge, I place Margot back on her feet and drop down onto one knee. "This isn't how I planned to do it but seeing you inside now smiling brightly, I couldn't wait any longer. The ring is at home but, Margot, I don't want to go another day without you by my side. From that first fake moment, our fate was sealed. And now that I have you, I don't ever want to be without you. So, what do you say? Do you want to be my wife?"

She stands above me, staring wide-eyed. Not saying anything. I have no clue what she's going to say.

The hours, well, it feels like hours, tick by and then she drops to her knees in front of me, grips my cheeks, and slams her lips to mine. "Yes," she murmurs against my lips. "Yes, I'll marry you."

Then she's kissing me again.

Wrapping my arms around her, I hold her tightly and seal our engagement with a kiss. Pulling back, I rest my forehead against hers. "I love you, Margot Radclyff. You've made me the happiest man in the world."

"And you've made me the happiest woman in the world, Jett. Life with you has been perfectly perfect, and I cannot wait to spend the rest of my days with you as my husband. I love you so fucking much."

And like the last wedding we attended, we left before the bride and groom to have our own private celebration for two.

Sitting in the back of the taxi, I look over at my fiancée, feeling as happy as the day I was drafted to the Crushers.

When I was trying out for the big league, my dad said, "Son, fake it till you make it," and that's exactly what I did; then and now. We may have started off as fake, but now that my ring is on her finger—well, it will be once we get home and I slide it onto her finger—it's real. As Chelsea would say, it's so pucking real and I'm never letting her go ... ever!

THE PUCKING END!

Want to know more about how Kallen and Chelsea fell in love? You can in I Pucking Hate That I Love You.

I vowed I'd never give my heart to another hockey player again. I learned my lesson the first time. But then I met Kallen Jones and he became a huge problem.

Not only is he on my "Don't Fall in Love with A Hockey Player" list, but he's also sitting pretty high on my "I want you" list. But I can't date a puckhead again.

It doesn't matter how good looking he is with his blue eyes, lickable abs, and heart of gold. He's a hockey player and my dad is his coach. Except Kallen isn't like the others. He treats me like a princess and has me doubting my decision and breaking my vow at every turn.

Until he turns out to be just like the last puckhead I
gave my heart to.

I pucking hate him but I also pucking love him…I'm so
pucking screwed.

The Heart Wants What It Wants - Selena Gomez
Valentine - 5 Seconds of Summer
Can't Help Falling in Live - Elvis Presley
With Or Without You - U2
Rewrite The Stars - Zac Efron, Zendaya
Need You Now - Lady A
She Will Be Loves - Maroon 5
Kiss Me - Ed Sheeran
If I Could Fly - One Direction
Just Give Me a Reason - P!nk, Nate Reuss
Fallin' In Love - Shawn Mendes
When I Look At You - Miley Cyrus
Perfectly Perfect - Simple Plan
You & I - One Direction
FAKE LOVE - BTS
Everything Has Changed - Taylor Swift, Ed Sheeran
Million Reasons - Lady Gaga
Stay With Men - Sam Smith
Wannabe - Spice Girls

This playlist can be found on Spotify.

ACKNOWLEDGMENTS

These things never get any easier and I always feel like I've forgotten someone so this is a blanket thank you to everyone who I have crossed paths with on this authoring journey.

Karen Hrdlicka from **Barren Acres Editing**; thank you for everything that you do for me.

Lisa; thank you for checking all my I's are dotted, my T's are crossed and there's no extra e's or s's.

Renae from **R.L Cover Designs**; once again, I gave to an image and a colour and BOOM, you nailed it. Big thank you for allowing the million and one tweaks when it came to the right shade of pink... who knew there were so many hues.

Kristy from **Vanilla Lily**; thank you for another gorgeous cover. As soon as I saw this set, I had to have them and with the little tweaks they are now perfect.

My beta babes **Bec, Lana, Margaret and Sarah;** I would be lost without you ladies. You give me advice when I second guess everything and you helped to bring this story to life. Thank you from the bottom of my heart.

Troy, my husband, my everything. You really are awesome at what you do and you're an even better husband and father. Love you long-time dude.

To my munchkins, **Piper** and **Kade**. You two are my greatest achievement and I'm so lucky to have you both in my life. Love you long-time guys and I look forward to the day when you are forty and can finally read my books.

And finally, **you, my reader**. Thanks for taking a chance on this hockey book and me. This series was only meant to be a standalone but it's now a 7 book series cause you guys loved Kallen and Chels just as much as I did. I cannot wait for you guys to meet the rest of the Pucking crew.

Cheers,
Dana XoXoX

ALSO BY DL GALLIE

STAND ALONES

Antecedent

Doc Steel

Oops

Off the Books

Out of Nowhere

Deck...the Balls

Secrets and Sunrises

Always in the Cards

Fractured

The Christmas Ornament

Before the Ashes

After the Ashes

Love Me Like You Do

Never Let Me Go

Seven Nights

Seven Kisses

PUCKING LOVE SERIES

I Pucking Hate That I Love You

A Pucking Good Christmas

I Pucking Hate That You Love Me

I Pucking Hate To Love You

It's Pucking Fake

...and a few pucking more

FALLING NOVELS

These men make it hard not to fall for them

Falling for Dr. Kelly

Falling for Dr. Knight

Falling for Agent Cox

Falling for Agent Cruz

Falling: The Complete Collection

LORDS OF CRESTWOOD PREP

Co-write with Tara Lee

Thatcher

Reign

Hendrix

Saint

THE UNEXPECTED SERIES

When it comes to love, expect the unexpected

The Unexpected Gift

The Unexpected Letter

The Unexpected Package

The Unexpected Connection

The Unexpected series: The Complete Collection

THE LIQUOR CABINET SERIES

Liquor has never been so disturbingly saucy

Malt Me (Book 1)

Tequila Healing (Book 2)

Wine Not (Book 3)

The Final Shot (Book 4)

The Liquor Cabinet: Series boxset

All of these books are available on Amazon.

FACEBOOK ~ INSTAGRAM ~ BOOKBUB

GOODREADS ~ WEBSITE

dlgallieauthor@outlook.com

Sign up to my newsletter

ABOUT THE AUTHOR

DL Gallie is from Queens-
land, Australia, but she's
lived in many different
places all over the world,
including the UK and
Canada. She currently
resides in Central Queens- 
land with her husband and two munchkins. She and
her husband have been together since she was
sixteen, and although they drive each other crazy at
times, she couldn't imagine her life without him.

Shortly after her son was born, DL began reading
again. With encouragement from her husband, she
picked up the pen and started writing, and now the
voices in her head won't shut up.

DL enjoys listening to music, drinking white wine in
the summer, red wine in the winter, and beer all year

round. She's also never been known to turn down a cocktail, especially a margarita.